**Harry** and **Alphonso**
(The Sunnytown firemen)

**Freda** and **Bobby** and **Olivia** and **Bert**
(From Sunnytown garage)

**François** and **Agatha**
(They deliver the post)

**Mr McGregor** and **Rose**
(They grow lots of plants)

**Mr** and **Mrs Smudge** and **Scruff**
(The messiest family in town)

**Daisy** and **Felix** and **Amit**
(They sell sandwiches, carpets and rugs)

**Otto**
and **Robin**

**Indira**
and **Flopsy** and **Tiny Mouse**

**Monsieur Pompidou** and **Signor Uffizzi**
(The museum curators)

**Lenny**
(He sweeps up)

**Isabella** and **Audrey**
(The traffic police lady and police horse)

**Noriko**
(The local photographer)

**Sydney** and **Lily** and **Florence**
(He cleans the windows and Florence bakes the bread)

# Migloo's Weekend

## by **william bee**

It's Saturday morning! Migloo is up nice and early and he's ready for his breakfast!

"Mrs Luigi's new cafe opens today, Migloo! Would you like a lift?" says Noah. Migloo wags his tail, ever such a lot, which means, 'I certainly do! I've been looking forward to it, ever such a lot!'

## AT THE MARKET

Oh dear, just look at that queue!
Migloo is far too hungry to wait! Luckily, his
friend Hannah comes to the rescue.
"Come on, Migloo, I know somewhere where
they do a very good breakfast!"
Migloo wags his tail, which means, 'LET'S GO!'

# AT SUNNYTOWN FARM

Look! It's Sunnytown Farm! There's Reg picking up some freshly picked, crunchy carrots; Mr Luigi collecting tubs of lovely fresh dairy cream, and – YUCK! There's the pong of Audrey and Maria's freshly-made manure! But where is Farmer Tom? And, more importantly, *where* is Migloo's breakfast?

**COMBINE HARVESTER**

# SUNNYTOWN FARM

*There's Farmer Tom!*

He's ready for his breakfast, too! "So, Migloo, what will it be? Sausages? Eggs? Bacon? Creamy, fruity yoghurt?" Migloo finds it awfully hard to choose so opts for ... *all* of them.

After breakfast, Migloo bumps into Isabella and Roshan.

TRAFFIC POLICE

"Look, Migloo!" says Isabella. "We're learning to ride our new police horses!" Migloo doesn't know much about horse riding, but he's pretty sure one of them is doing *something* wrong.

There's drama in the pigsty! Last week, Rosie had nine little piglets. But Hannah and Suki can only count eight! "Have you seen Pigwig, Migloo?" Migloo doesn't wag his tail, which means, 'I'm not saying anything...'

Well, what a lovely start to Migloo's weekend. And now Miss Othmar offers Migloo a ride in the school's shiny new minibus. Migloo wags his tail, which means, 'Yes please! As long as it doesn't break down like the old one...'

# AT SUNNYTOWN MUSEUM

**P**hew! They've made it – all the way to Sunnytown Museum. Migloo LOVES the museum. It's full of all sorts of wonderful THINGS! There are big things, really big things, old things, really old things, and scary things like ... the really BIG, really OLD, really SCARY *Tyrannosaurus rex!*

**? QUESTION TIME ?**

Can you see a rubber duck?
Who's on a ladder?
Can you find Parrot?
And who's reading?

WORLD REC

**But Migloo isn't scared! He's hungry!**

He's not scared of that stuffed shark
with its mouth full of sharp, pointy teeth ...

or the old cannon with its big,
heavy cannonballs ...

or *even*
the giant's GIGANTIC marble foot.

But he *is* a bit scared of Monsieur
Pompidou and Signor Uffizzi, the
museum curators, so he gives
them back their dinosaur bone.

Lenny has spent ALL DAY scrubbing the steam engine. But, oh dear! He really should have done it AFTER Mr Smudge cleaned out the chimney!

Migloo is now covered head to toe in sooty soot. He needs a nice, bubbly bath! Harry and Alphonso are outside and they're happy to help.
But it takes so long to get Migloo clean that they're going to be late! "Come on, Migloo! Jump on board! We're off to..."

## AT SUNNYTOWN CINEMA

### THE MOVIES!

Everyone finds a place to sit and something tasty to eat, all ready to watch the latest FLASHY GORDON MOVIE!

This time, Flashy is trying to protect the earth from a couple of greedy green Martians who have hatched a terrible plan...

FLASHY GORDON

The Martians have come to eat up all of Earth's nicest food!
Like our juicy oranges and sweet, crunchy carrots and
delicious oaties and lovely lickable ice creams and
mouthwatering apples and super sizzling sausages!

It's a HORROR movie!

There's only one thing to do – Migloo MUST eat as much as he possibly can, before it's too late!

The film is over! In the end, the greedy Martians felt *very sick*, and went home *very* quickly. Migloo would like to go home, too, but Olivia wants him to go to her house for a Saturday night sleepover. Migloo wags his tail very weakly, which means, 'Yes please, as long as I don't have to eat anything else...'

Well, what a busy Saturday!
Time for a story and time for bed.

Lily is already asleep, dreaming about horses.

Felix is dreaming about scoring a goal for Sunnytown United.

Lotti and Toto cannot sleep as their dad is reading from his big book of Viking legends, and their mum is noisily acting them out.

Hulot's dad is busy blowing up balloons. You can NEVER have enough balloons!

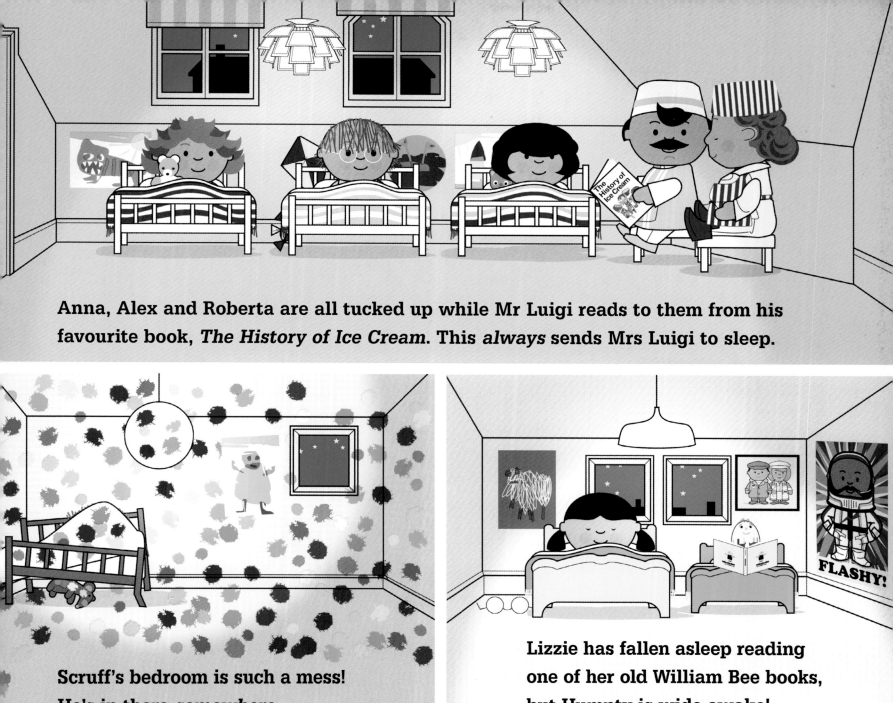

Anna, Alex and Roberta are all tucked up while Mr Luigi reads to them from his favourite book, *The History of Ice Cream*. This *always* sends Mrs Luigi to sleep.

Scruff's bedroom is such a mess! He's in there *somewhere*...

Lizzie has fallen asleep reading one of her old William Bee books, but Humpty is wide awake!

And Migloo curls up between Olivia's bed and baby Bobby's cot.

"Good night, Migloo," says Olivia.

# Race Day in Sunnytown!

It's Sunday morning ... RACE DAY!
After a long sleep and a breakfast of tea
and cereal and jam on toast, Migloo grabs a
spanner and sets off to help Bert and Freda
and Olivia. It's going to be a very busy day ...
they're the only mechanics in town!

Mrs Dickens doesn't actually know how to drive a racing car, but that's OK, she's got a book – *How to Drive a Racing Car Without Hitting Anything.*

Migloo's been so busy being a mechanic ...

that he's forgotten to have his lunch!
So he makes a quick pit stop with Daisy,
Felix and Amit for a sandwich.

Uh-oh! Suki can't get her racing car to start, not *even* with
Bert and Freda and Olivia helping.
But she's had an idea!

"Quick, Tom! Quick, Migloo! Help me take all the go-faster
bits off my racing car ... and we'll put them on my Super
Sizzling Sausage car!" Migloo wags his tail, which means,
'Good thinking, Suki!'

# AT THE STARTING LINE

Suki's Sausage car really does look like a racing car now! "Do you want to come for a ride, Migloo?" she asks.

Migloo slowly wags his tail, which means, 'OK. But are you *sure* this thing is safe?!' The lights are red... The lights are green... *GO! GO! GO!* Suki races away in a cloud of flames, smoke and sizzling sausages!

## QUESTION TIME

Can you spot Batty?
Who has an orange juice?
Can you see Little White Owl?

So who is Sunnytown's racing champion?
Is it Amit with his six-wheeled racer? Or Reg in his vegetable-green Racing Machine? Or Mrs Dickens or Flossy or Terry?

No! It's Suki in her cobbled-together-at-the-last-minute, hang-on-tight, Super-Sizzling-Sausage-Speed-machine!

Migloo's head is spinning! He's NEVER getting in a car with Suki again – sausages or no sausages!

Everyone hurries to pack up the cars and tyres,
the spanners, the fuel cans and jacks,
because the weekend isn't over yet!

There's still one more exciting place to go...

SUNNYTOWN FAIR! A helter-skelter! A haunted house!
Balloons and bumper cars! Popcorn and candyfloss!
And most exciting of all? The fair is going to be
opened by a world-famous film star ...

*FLASHY GORDON!*

# AT THE FUNFAIR

**YES!** Flashy Gordon!
Wait – NO Flashy Gordon?!
**Where IS Flashy Gordon?!**
*"WE CAN'T START WITHOUT*
*FLASHY GORDON!"*
No one knows what to do! But Migloo – who has had a lovely weekend being driven about by all his friends, and being fed sausages and eggs and bacon and creamy, fruity yoghurt and ice creams and jam on toast –

has spotted something ...

Thanks to Migloo, the great Flashy Gordon is rescued!
Sunnytown Fair is a whirr of bright colours and spinning carousels.
Migloo happily wags his tail, which means, 'Now I feel like a flashy
film star, too!'

? QUESTION ?
TIME
Can you see Chameleon?
What have the
two toucans taken?
Where is that leprech

SUNNYTOWN NEWS

FLASHY SAVED
BY MIGLOO!

READ ALL ABOUT IT!

SUNN
Lights to be switched on
by FAMOUS FILM STAR!
WN
NYTOWN PARK
.50 CHILDREN GO FREE

FLASHY GORDON
HERE TONIGHT!

TRAFFIC

For:
Flashy

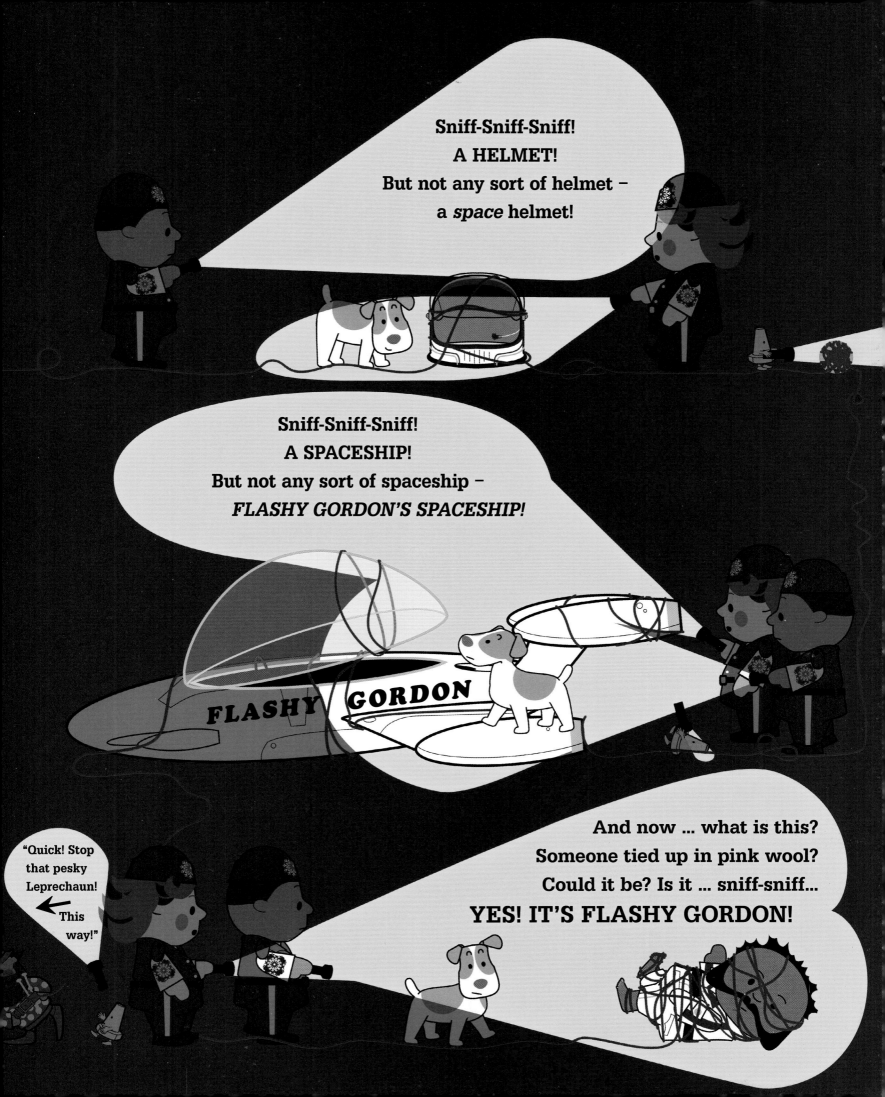

# William Bee's Busy Page

Sunnytown is such a busy place, *especially* at the weekend. There are lots and lots of people out and about shopping, eating, driving, playing and seeing the sights, which means ... there are lots and lots of things for YOU to look out for!

## Look at all these logos. Whose are they?

1  2  3  4

5  6  7

8

ANSWERS: 1. The Post Office's 2. Eric and Ernie's Building Services' 3. Sunnytown Museum's 4. The Fire Station's 5. Elephant Petrol's 6. Sunnytown Carpets' 7. Noah the fisherman's 8. Hannah the vet's

## Who's hiding in Zebedee's dressing up car?

ANSWERS: Parrot, Robin, Indira, Batty, Owl, Chameleon, Little White Mouse, Gwendolyn (or is it Cecily?), Penguin, Flopsy, Grey Squirrel, Cecily (or is it Gwendolyn?), Crabby, Little Brown Mouse and Red Squirrel.

## Who's going racing?

1

2

3

4

5

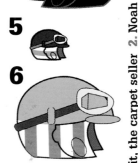
6

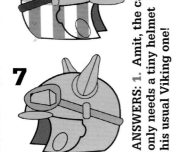
7

ANSWERS: 1. Amit, the carpet seller 2. Noah 3. Reg, who sells the veg 4. William Bee 5. Henrietta Hen, who only needs a tiny helmet 6. Flossy, the candyfloss and popcorn lady 7. Noggin, in his racing helmet, and not his usual Viking one!

## There are 25 toy Martians to find. Have you spotted them all?

(Including this one!)

## Noriko is always taking photos. Can you find where she took these?

ANSWERS: 1. At the race starting line – there's Juan nearly getting squashed 2. At the cinema – popcorn calamity! 3. In the museum ... Maria has made a mess! 4. At the market, there's trouble when Otto stands on Noggin's Plinth!

## Who's moustache is Migloo wearing?

1

2

3

4

5

6

ANSWERS: 1. Charlie, the newspaper man's 2. Noggin, the Viking's 3. Farmer Tom's 4. Mr Brush, the musical brush seller's 5. Amit, the carpet seller's 6. Flashy Gordon's – what a flashy tashy!

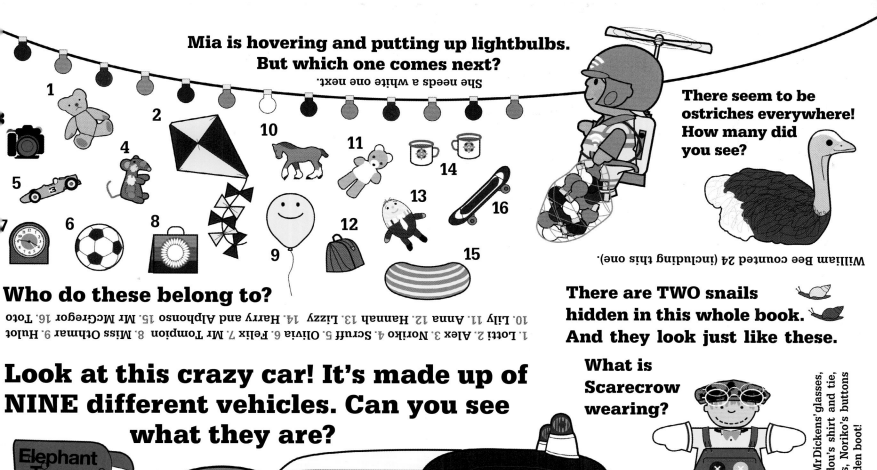

## Mia is hovering and putting up lightbulbs. But which one comes next?

She needs a white one next.

1
2
10
11
14
4
5
3
13
16
7
6
8
12
9
15

**There seem to be ostriches everywhere! How many did you see?**

William Bee counted 24 (including this one).

## Who do these belong to?

1. Lotti 2. Alex 3. Noriko 4. Scruff 5. Olivia 6. Felix 7. Mr Tompion 8. Miss Othmar 9. Hulot 10. Lily 11. Anna 12. Hannah 13. Lizzy 14. Harry and Alphonso 15. Mr McGregor 16. Toto

**There are TWO snails hidden in this whole book. And they look just like these.**

## Look at this crazy car! It's made up of NINE different vehicles. Can you see what they are?

**Elephant Tyres**

**FISH**

**What is Scarecrow wearing?**

MrSmudge'shat, MrDickens' glasses, Monsieur Pompidou's shirt and tie, Boris's dungarees, Noriko's buttons and Noggin's golden boot!

The blue racing wing is from Amit's racing car. It's attached to the back of Bert and Freda's tow truck. Underneath is Sydney's motorbike sidecar. Those great big wheels are from Sunnytown Museum's steam engine. The windows are from the school minibus, and the front door is from Noah's car. The cab is from the fire engine. The front is from Hannah's car and right at the front is the pointy nose of Sunnytown School's racing car.

## Busy Bee Questions

**How many times can you spot Roberta's little wheelie cat?**

We counted 12 times (including this one).

Here are all the things to find and how many times to find them in total!

On the pages where you see William Bee holding his yellow "QUESTION TIME" sign, it means there are LOTS of things to find!

And if you feel like getting even BUSIER, you can find the answers to ALL the questions he asks below on EACH and EVERY one of the 7 pages where his yellow "QUESTION TIME" sign appears!

So, that means: you can find Flopsy 7 times and find a missing shoe in 7 different places! And lots of people eating carrots, wearing glasses and swapping hats! Phew … that IS busy!

Who's reading? (14) Who's on a ladder? (21) Who's holding a spanner? (24) Who has lost a shoe? (7) Who's holding a lolly or ice cream? (40) Who has a carrot? (29) Who's wearing glasses? (71) Apart from Mr Tati and Hulot, who's holding a balloon? (8) And who has an orange juice? (27) **CAN YOU SEE:** Migloo? (7) Tiny White Mouse and Tiny Brown Mouse? (7 each) A rubber duck? (7) An ostrich egg? (12) Cecily and Gwendolyn? (7 each) Indira? (7) Batty? (7) Red Squirrel and Grey Squirrel? (7 each) Little White Owl? (7) Penguin? (7) Mr Smudge – usually just his sooty brush? (7) Flopsy? (7) Parrot? (7) Robin? (7) Chameleon? (7) The pesky leprechaun? (7) Who has swapped hats? What do Mr Tati's balloons spell? What's the time? What have the two toucans taken?

# Goodbye, Migloo.

## See you again soon.

First published 2016 by Walker Books Ltd, 87 Vauxhall Walk, London SE11 5HJ • © 2016 William Bee • 10 9 8 7 6 5 4 3 2 1 • **The** right of **W**illiam Bee **t**o be identified as author/illustrator of this work has been asserte**d b**y him in **a**cco**r**dance with the Copyright, Designs and Patents Act 1988 • This boo**k** ha**s** been typeset in UR**W** Egypt**i**enne, Cooper Five Op**t**i Black, VAG Rounded, Eurostile, Helvetica, Textile • Printed in China • All rights
British Library Catal**o**guing in Publication Data: a catalog**u**e record for this book is available from the British Library • ISBN 978-1-4063-3931-4 • www.walker.co.uk

**www.mig14ooworld.com** **migloo**